Crabs for Dinner

Story by
Adwoa Badoe

Art by
Belinda Ageda

Sister Vision
Black Women and Women of Colour Press

Canadian Cataloguing in Publication Data
Badoe, Adwoa
Crabs for Dinner

ISBN 0-920813-27-5

I. Ageda, Belinda.II. Title.

PS8553.A3607   1995   jC813'.54   C95-932500-X
                           PZ7.B33Cr   1995

Story edited by Robert Munsch

Production and Design: Stephanie Martin
Editor for the Press: Makeda Silvera
Printed in Canada by Metrolitho

*Sister Vision Press acknowledges the financial support of the Canada
Council and the Ontario Arts Council towards its publishing program.*

*Represented in Canada by the Literary Press Group
Distributed by General Distribution*

SISTER VISION
Black Women and Women of Colour Press
P.O. Box 217, Station E
Toronto, Ontario
Canada M6H 4E2

For Wynne, Matthew and Stephanie

A.B.

To a crab named Sonia and my family
at home and abroad

B.A.

I do not like crab.
I do not like fufu.
I do not like palm nut soup.

My sister Emily does not like crab.
She does not like fufu.
She does not like palm nut soup.

So when my aunties and uncle come to dinner we eat
chicken or french fries or pizza or hamburgers
and we never touch the stuff the
grownups are eating.

They eat crabs. Big grey crabs with orange tipped pincers that Mum buys from the African shop. She makes soup with palm nut and crabs. The grownups eat the soup along with soft balls of potato fufu.

"Mmm," Aunt Pauline said to my mum.

"No one makes crab and fufu quite like you do."

"Delicious, simply delicious," Uncle Robert said between mouthfuls of potato fufu.

My Aunt Araba's sucking and crunching sound said it all for her.

"Disgusting," Emily whispered behind Mummy's back.

"Yuk," I whispered.

One summer, my grandmother came for a visit all the way from Africa.

"Ghana," she said. "That's where I come from."
She brought us funny-looking clothes, the kind they wear in
Ghana. I had a smock made of a rough cotton fabric with stripes of
bright colours woven into it.

It was long and loose, almost like a
dress. Grandma said it was meant to be
worn over a pair of trousers.

"I'm never
going to
wear
those,"
I said to
my mum.

But Emily wore hers,
a colourful batik dress
with embroidery
around the neck.

She looked so pretty that I decided to wear my smock. When I did, I thought I looked "cool". Especially when I wore the striped cotton cap that came with the smock.

Grandma had lots of stories to
tell. Stories her grandmother
told her when she was young.
I liked the ones about a
cunning "Spider man"
who got in and out
of all kinds of
trouble.

stuck to the tar dwarf, was own Ananse in his Sunday best.

She always ended in a funny way, saying:
"This story of mine whether good or bad, may pass away, or come to stay. It is your turn to tell your story."

So we took our turn and told her stories. And she liked them just as much as we liked hers.

A week before she left for Ghana, she invited my aunts and uncle to dinner.

"She's going to make soup and yucky crab," Emily said. "I'll bet she makes a lot of it. But I won't even take a bite."

She did make the soup, only she put in okra too.

"That's going to make it slimy," I said.

"Double Yuk," said Emily.

But dinner got cooked and dinner was served and grace was said.

Emily and I were eating hot dogs and the grownups were eating slime.

Uncle Robert rolled his eyes upwards.
"Mmm," he said. "Exquisite!"

I had
never
heard him
use that word
for Mum's soup.

"My word," Aunt Pauline said, "I had almost forgotten the original taste."

My mum simply said,
"Delicious."

Even Aunt Araba paused from the sucking and crunching to say one word,

"Authentic!"

I noticed that Grandma's soup smelled really good, much better than Mum's soup. Suddenly I wanted to taste just a little bit of the fufu with crab and soup.

"Can I have a little please?"
I heard Emily ask.

"Why, of course!" Grandma replied.

If Emily doesn't die I'll have some,
I thought.

Emily took a bite and didn't die.
Instead she took another bite.

"And how about you?" said
Grandma.

"Yes please," I said.

It tasted different, not like the soups I knew. It was spicy and hot and really good. It was thick and smooth and I thought I could taste the flavour of ginger.

I broke off a tiny
piece of crab and
sucked it just like
Mummy did. It was
all soft inside.
Then I crunched
on it, really hard,
just as my Aunt
Araba did.

Then I ate a whole
bowl of fufu and
soup and a huge
piece of crab.

When I was done I rolled my eyes up to the sky and said aloud, "Exquisite!"

I am not even sure what that means, but probably it is a way of saying that sometimes grandmothers cook better than mothers.

Adwoa Badoe was born in Ghana, West Africa, where she qualified as a physician in 1988. Since becoming a mother, she has developed a keen interest in children's literature. She spends much of her time writing down the stories she tells her son. She currently lives in Canada.

Belinda Ageda is a multi-talented visual artist enjoying a successful career as an illustrator of books. She has also explored such creative avenues as scenic paintings for theatre. Her work has been praised for its sincerity and humour.